LEGO NINJAGO

5-MINUTE STORIES

LEGO NINJAGO
5-MINUTE STORIES

Random House 🏠 New York

Illustrated by AMEET Studio

AMEET Sp. z o.o.
Nowe Sady 6, 94-102 Łódź—Poland
Published in the United States by Random House Children's Books, a division of
Penguin Random House LLC, 1745 Broadway, New York, NY 10019, and in Canada by
Penguin Random House Canada Limited, Toronto. Random House and the colophon
are registered trademarks of Penguin Random House LLC.
rhcbooks.com
ISBN 978-0-593-38138-0 (trade) — ISBN 978-0-593-38139-7 (ebook)
PRINTED IN CHINA
10 9 8 7 6 5 4 3 2 1

CONTENTS

ENTER THE WORLD OF SPINJITZU

Master Wu is an expert in the art of **Spinjitzu**. In his younger days, he was a fierce warrior, schooled in the ways of the ninja. Master Wu is confident that all his students can learn, but he knows that it takes time, patience, and wisdom to truly master Spinjitzu. He also knows that to protect the Ninjago world, there are sacrifices that only he must bear.

NINJA MISSION

As the time for the ultimate battle between good and evil approaches, Master Wu must deal with another battle—the one that rages inside him.

Jay, the fast Lightning Ninja.

Kai, the hot-headed Fire Ninja.

Nya, the Water Ninja, and Kai's brave sister.

Cole, the strong Earth Ninja.

Zane the Nindroid, the intelligent Ice Ninja.

Lloyd, wise Master of Energy.

He suspects there may still be some good left in his evil brother and enemy, Lord Garmadon, but he fears that he may have to destroy him before that goodness can be reached. Helping him in this battle are his students.

Not so long ago . . .
and closer than you might think,
in the world of Ninjago . . .

The ninja were called before their master. Wu sat on the floor in the Monastery of Spinjitzu, drinking tea and looking at his pupils in silence. Kai cleared his throat, but the silence continued until the master had finished his tea. Then he finally spoke.

"Ninja, I need you to bring this very important package to

Ninjago City for me," Wu said. "Place it in the dojo there and guard it until tomorrow. Guard it carefully. Do not let it fall into enemy hands!"

"We won't fail you, Master Wu!" Lloyd promised. Jay, Kai, Nya, Cole, and Zane nodded in agreement.

The six ninja raced out of the Monastery of Spinjitzu into the mysterious and dangerous areas of Ninjago that led to the city. Enemies lurked behind every tree and bush, and the forces of darkness followed their every footstep.

"We need to remain cautious," ordered Lloyd. "Evildoers could be out there, just waiting to steal the package."

The Green Ninja was right. At that very moment, they were being secretly watched by three skeletons.

As the ninja disappeared around a bend, the skeletons followed them.

But there was something even more surprising. . . .

The skeletons were being followed by the Serpentine, who were in turn being spied on from the bushes by two Stone Warriors! All the villains knew they were no match for the six ninja, but they followed them anyway, hoping for a chance to strike.

After a few miles, the ninja reached the outskirts of Ninjago City. Because ninja were trained not to rest during missions—especially ones as important as this—they kept up their fast pace.

"We're almost there," said Kai. "Good work, everyone!"

"Let's race!" Cole shouted suddenly. "The last one to the dojo does the dishes after dinner!"

The ninja ran along the cluttered city streets. Cole was in the lead, but the others were gaining quickly.

"Why don't they slow down a bit?" one of the skeletons said, panting. "I'm tired already!"

"Even if I had lungs, I wouldn't be able to catch my breath," the other skeleton added.

Finally reaching their destination, the ninja ran into the dojo in Ninjago City.

"Let's hide the package," Nya suggested. "The dojo is loaded with awesome security. It'll be safe until Master Wu arrives."

"Sounds good to me," Jay said as his stomach rumbled loud enough for everyone to hear. "But that doesn't! Let's grab something to eat."

Little did the ninja know, the skeletons were waiting for them to leave the room. The villains could see through the large windows where the Masters of Spinjitzu hid the package.

"It's ours now!" one of the skeletons said, and laughed so hard that he almost fell off the roof.

Two Skulkin warriors snuck quietly into the dojo. The bony bad guys quickly located the package in its hiding spot and carried it away. Thinking their task was complete, the Skulkin cackled happily, until . . . THUMP! One of them fell through a trapdoor and landed right on a table—where the ninja were relaxing!

"Intruders!" Zane exclaimed.

"My noodles!" Jay cried.

Cole ran to the window. He saw the other skeleton warrior running away with the package—leaping from rooftop to rooftop.

"Stop right now, you numbskull!" Cole yelled.

The ninja raced out of the dojo. WHOOSH! They released their elemental powers and set off in pursuit of the Skulkin, spinning along the rooftops in whirlwinds.

"Everything is going according to plan," Lloyd whispered to Kai as they ran after one of the Skulkin.

The skeleton warrior was fast, but he tripped over a slippery snake tail. The package flew out of his hands . . . and right into the hands of a Serpentine, who had waited patiently to trip him!

"The package is *oursssss* now!" the Serpentine
hissed as he and his reptilian accomplice dashed away.
But they didn't get far.

Suddenly, a group of Stone Warriors surrounded
the Serpentine! One of the Stone Warriors snatched
the package away from the Serpentine and
disappeared over the rooftop faster than anyone
believed a stone warrior could run.

The ninja chased the Stone Warriors deep into the darkest parts of the city. Then they followed them into what had to be one of the creepiest hideouts ever. The ninja burst through the door and found themselves face to face with Lord Garmadon!

"Garmadon!" Lloyd shouted. "But how?"

Lord Garmadon laughed at the sight of the six ninja.

"I have spies everywhere," Garmadon gloated. "And what I don't already know, they tell me. So I knew all about your little ninja mission as soon as you stepped out of your temple."

Lord Garmadon yanked the package from the Stone Warrior's hands and sneered at the ninja. "Now let's find out what my dearest brother had you guard so carefully. . . ."

Excited, Garmadon quickly opened the box—POOF!

Confetti and packing foam exploded from the package—but that was it! Garmadon dug into the box. There was nothing inside. It was empty!

"SURPRISE!" the ninja shouted.

Garmadon was speechless.

"Gotcha!" Cole added with a chuckle.

Garmadon scowled.

"WHAT IS THE MEANING OF THIS?" he roared.

"The package was only bait," explained Lloyd. "Master Wu knew you'd send your goons to steal it. We let them, and they led us back to your hideout. Back to you. Now you're coming with us!"

"Looks like you are the only one leaving empty-handed," said Jay.

"Justice is served," added Kai. "Three cheers for Master Wu!"

THE EVIL ENGAGEMENT

By Greg Farshtey

When an evil djinn named **Nadakhan** appears—freed from the teapot that had imprisoned him for ages—he immediately gets up to no good. The djinn has the ability to grant wishes, but they always turn against the wisher. The ninja make a BIG mistake when they wish for the power to defeat him! Now Nya is on the verge of becoming Nadakhan's bride, only a handful of ninja are left to fight the djinn, and, most important to this particular story, **Clancee** the peg-legged Serpentine pirate has to figure out how to bake a wedding cake. . . .

"There is going to be a wedding," Nadakhan announced to his assembled crew. "Make the necessary preparations."

The crew of the flying pirate ship *Misfortune's Keep* glanced at each other as their djinn captain stalked away. Everyone knew they had to obey orders and help make the wedding between Nadakhan and Nya a success. They also knew what would happen to them if the ceremony was a failure. Nadakhan wasn't known as the forgiving type, so no one wanted to be the first to volunteer to be wedding planner. Well, almost no one . . .

"Wow! Romantic!"

Clancee cried, hopping around on his wooden leg. "I haven't been to a wedding since . . . since . . . actually, I've never been to a wedding. But I bet they're fun!"

Flintlocke, the djinn's trusted first mate, and Dogshank, a hulking brute, looked at each other with big smiles creeping onto their faces. It looked like they had found their wedding planner.

Clancee was excited about being given the job of organizing the big event.

Sure, there were challenges, like the bride hating the groom. But all weddings came with minor obstacles, or so he had heard. The first thing he had to do, he decided, was make a list.

"Music, food, Nya's dress," he said, jotting them down on his list. "Oh, and a cake. Can't forget that."

The dress was easy. Nadakhan insisted on Nya wearing his mother's wedding gown. It had four sleeves, but that could be fixed.

Since the groom was much too busy to talk to him, Clancee decided to discuss arrangements with the bride. . . .

"What kind of flowers would you like?" he asked Nya.

"Stinkweed," she replied.

"Is there anyone I should leave off the guest list?"

"Yes—the groom."

"What do you want as a wedding gift?"

"To skip this wedding," Nya snarled.

It appeared that the bride was not going to be much help either, so Clancee went to check on how the preparations were going. Bucko (whose real name was Collin, but that's not a very pirate name), Flintlocke, and some of the other pirates were busy transforming the interior of the Djinn Temple into a wedding chamber. Clancee marked it off his to-do list and left them to their work. He headed for the ship's kitchen galley.

It was time to make the wedding cake.

Clancee had been hoping Doubloon would be free to help him. It was true that Doubloon didn't know how to cook, but he had once robbed a baker, so that gave him more experience in the kitchen than any of the other pirates. But Doubloon was busy stealing the music for the ceremony. Baking the cake was going to be up to Clancee.

"No problem. I've got this," the little green pirate said confidently.

He raided the shops for all the ingredients he thought should go in a cake: flour, eggs, milk, sugar, peppers, chicken, barbecue sauce, a loaf of bread, and just a hint of lime. He mixed them all up in a pot and hung the pot over a fire.

"Now I just need to let this cook for six hours and I'm done!" Clancee said happily. It was almost time for the wedding rehearsal, so he left the galley to check on how the other preparations were coming along.

Doubloon had returned with the music. It took Clancee a long time to find something he liked. Most of the songs were about raiding small towns or sacking merchant ships. Sadly, there just weren't that many pirate love songs.

Clancee finally picked a sea shanty that sounded vaguely ceremonial and didn't have lyrics about stealing and firing cannons.

Clancee was about practice conducting the wedding ceremony when he was distracted by a wonderful smell. The cake! He rushed belowdecks to see how his creation was doing.

As he was rounding the corner to the galley, he collided with something soft and spongy that bounced him up against a wall.

The pirate's eyes went wide. The hallway was filled with cake from floor to ceiling! The stuff was growing by the minute, moving farther and farther down the passage. Something about his recipe had gone very wrong, he decided.

"Probably too much chicken," Clancee said.

There was only one thing to do. He drew his sword and attacked. Hacking and slashing, Clancee carved a path through the cake, trying to reach the galley. It was a hard-fought battle. Every time he thought he was on the verge of victory, the growing cake would close in around him again. At one point, he thought maybe he could eat his way through it, but he had been right the first time—there was way too much chicken.

"No baked good is going to stop me!" Clancee yelled, charging forward. Behind him, the cake was now starting to climb the stairs to the main deck. Unfortunately, it hadn't turned out to be very light and fluffy, so the weight was starting to drag *Misfortune's Keep* down.

At last, Clancee spotted the bubbling pot. He pushed his way through the sweet treat and yanked the pot off the cooking fire.

Now he just had to find a way to
explain all this to the others.

"What in the silver sea is going on here?"
bellowed Flintlocke. He was standing in the
door of the galley, covered in cake crumbs
and goo.

Clancee thought fast. "Um, a n-n-new n-ninja," he stuttered. "The Ninja of Cake. V-v-very dangerous. But no worries, I defeated him!"

Flintlocke hauled poor Clancee in front of Nadakhan.

As it turned out, the Ninja of Cake story did not go over well with the evil djinn.

"There'd better not be any more problems," Nadakhan demanded, his eyes pinning Clancee to the wall. **"Or it's going to be your head."**

Clancee kept that in mind later, when he began to conduct the ceremony. It wasn't exactly a dream wedding. The bride kept looking over her shoulder, hoping for rescue, and the groom was growing more and more enraged. But the music was nice, and the pieces of cake that Clancee had managed to save weren't too awful. Overall, as he reached the end of the service, Clancee was feeling pretty good about the job he had done.

"And under the watchful eye of this seventh sun, may this crown codify this renewal today, and for years to come," he said quickly, trying to make the marriage official before the djinn lost patience.

Suddenly, the sound of cannon fire came from outside the main doors. A minute later, the doors burst open to reveal the ninja team, reunited and ready for battle.

"And by the power vested in me," Clancee said, even faster, "I now pronounce you all-powerful."

Clancee dove under the nearest piece of furniture as the ninja confronted Nadakhan. The heroes were already realizing they were too late.

Nadakhan and Nya were married. Yuck!

Nadakhan quickly used his terrible magic to put his new bride to sleep as he turned to face the ninja.

"Oh, boy," thought Clancee. "Those ninja don't stand a chance. But if Nadakhan wins . . . what's going to happen to me?"

As Nadakhan created duplicates of himself to battle the heroes, Clancee went over in his mind all the little problems there had been at the wedding. Just the fact that the entire lower deck smelled of barbeque chicken and cake would probably be enough to get him banished forever. He had never seen the all-powerful djinn so angry, and it was a pretty scary sight.

He had to do something . . . but what? Get out of the temple and try to hide? Do something really heroic so Nadakhan wouldn't destroy him for at least another day or so? Or could he . . . would he . . . did he dare . . . help the ninja?

"Oh, no, I couldn't do that," Clancee said to himself.

"I'm a pirate! I plunder and loot, and I could never, um, never . . ."

A couple dozen duplicates of Nadakhans were now battling ninja all over the room. Holes were being blown in walls, pirates were being tossed through the air, and the djinn's dreadful laughter was ringing everywhere.

Clancee had to decide, but he couldn't. He sat down on the floor, covered in wedding cake, looked around at the wreckage of the wedding and the crazed djinn on a rampage, and wiped a tear from his eye.

"Now I g-get why people c-cry at weddings," Clancee sobbed.

WHAT GOES UP!

By Greg Farshtey

Jay assembles a group of . . . let's be nice and call them unique . . . warriors to help him save the world from Nadakhan, the evil wish–granting djinn. There is **Dareth**, who calls himself the Brown Ninja; **Skylor**, the reformed daughter of evil Master Chen—one of the ninjas' greatest enemies; **Captain Soto**, a pirate who fought Nadakhan in the distant past; **Ronin**, a professional thief; **Echo Zane**, a copy of one of Master Wu's ninja; and **Misako**—the mother of Lloyd, another of Wu's ninja. Will this diverse group of would-be heroes be enough to save the day? Let's find out. . . .

Master Wu looked up at the sky. The evil djinn Nadakhan had used his magic to lift huge chunks of earth and stone over the city. Even if the ninja won their fight against their enemy, the city was in danger of being crushed. Wu turned to the small group of warriors clustered around him. He sighed and shook his head.

"I have to remember to talk to Jay about team-building one day," Wu said to himself.

He hoped this motley crew of would-be heroes would be enough to save the day. If their hearts were in the right place and their courage held, anything was possible.

While the ninja were fighting to stop Nadakhan up in the sky on his flying pirate ship, Wu led this team to help the people on the ground.

"We all know what we have to do," Wu said to the group. "Let us be swift as a sparrow and mighty as a dragon."

"Well, I guess that's better than flat as a pancake," said Ronin.

Everyone knew it was a race against time. **If Nadakhan won, the world was doomed.**

If the ninja won, the city would be destroyed.

So if nothing else, they had to try to save the people in the city.

Dareth came upon a crowd of people on a street corner, frantically debating whether the world was coming to an end. He jumped on top of a car and said with a smile, "Cheer up, folks! The Brown Ninja is here to tell you everything is going to be OK."

The crowd quieted down, and someone said, "What's a brown ninja?"

"This!" said Dareth, going into a series of complicated martial arts moves. In minutes, the people who had been panicked before were smiling and applauding.

In another part of the city, Ronin and Echo Zane were keeping an eye out for anyone in need when they heard screams. Racing around the corner, they saw a building start to topple over.

"The ground beneath it must have been weakened after Nadakhan broke up the land and took it," said Zane the nindroid.

"Action first. Explain later," Ronin said, already on the run. He caught a flagpole and went into a rapid spin. When he had built up enough centrifugal force, he let go and rocketed toward the building. Timing it perfectly, he caught two people who were falling out of the building.

Meanwhile, Zane rushed over and used his amazing strength to slow the building's collapse long enough for rescue workers to evacuate the structure. Even Ronin was impressed.

And so it went, all over the city. Misako spoke with the commissioner, who dispersed police and firefighters to vulnerable points in the city. Captain Soto used a fisherman's net to haul in looters. Skylor helped save the city's power plant from an overload when half the facility got dragged into the sky by the djinn's magic.

Finally, when most of the people in the city were safe from immediate danger, the team reunited with Master Wu to check in and figure out what they needed to do next. No one could forget they were standing in the shadow of rock and earth hovering in the sky above them.

"We're doing all right so far," said Misako. **"But it's all for nothing if they don't win the battle up there."**

A sudden tremor shook the ground beneath the heroes' feet. Cracks began appearing in the street around where they were standing, spreading rapidly in every direction.

"I hate to tell you this," said Ronin, "but it may be all for nothing anyway!"

"Watch out!" yelled Dareth.

It was already too late. The slab of land they were
standing on broke free and soared into the air to
join all the others Nadakhan had stolen. Captain Soto
peered over the edge and saw more chunks of land
tearing themselves loose and rising toward the sky.

"Long way down," said Skylor. "And getting longer every second. Are we going to do something about this? The top floor is full of nasty pirates and an evil djinn."

Master Wu frowned. "We are rising quickly, and it is already too far for most of us to jump."

Echo Zane cut in. "Yes, a jump could result in multiple injuries, and—"

"We get the picture," interjected Ronin. "Maybe you could Spinjitzu us down, Wu?"

Master Wu shook his head. "I can't carry all of you to safety quickly enough."

Dareth looked up at the land mass that had formed in the sky from the stolen pieces of Ninjago terrain. Then he looked down and saw more hunks of earth and rock rising from the surface like a swarm of giant insects . . . or did they actually look more like stepping stones? The brown ninja smiled.

"That's our way out," he said, pointing downward. "We jump from one piece of land to the next until we reach the street. But we have to be fast and accurate, or else . . . **squish**."

"Squish?" repeated Echo Zane.

"Never mind," said Ronin. "It's a technical term."

"I don't have a better idea," said Skylor, "so I guess I'll go first."

With that, Skylor leapt off the edge. She dropped about two yards to the next floating hunk of rock. **"Nothing to it!"** Skylor yelled up to the others. "See you at the bottom!"

Ronin waited for her to make another jump before following. Dareth gave Captain Soto a little nudge toward the edge. "Don't worry, it's no harder than jumping from one ship to another in a storm."

"Aye," replied the old pirate. "And what crazy fools would ever do that?"

"Us!" said Dareth as he pushed the surprised captain in the direction of the next rock. Soto fell, flailing and yelling.

Echo Zane held out his hand to Misako. "Shall we?"

Skylor was finding it tough going. The pieces of land accelerated as they rose higher, making it hard to judge speed and distance. One time she almost tumbled off, and another time she skidded upon landing and barely held on. She was about to make the next jump when Ronin unexpectedly landed behind her.

"Problem?" he asked.

"I don't have problems," she replied, jumping off. **"I usually *cause* problems!"**

Knowing the thief was watching, Skylor flipped in midair, landed on her hands on the next rock, then pushed off and flipped again, effortlessly, to the ground. She looked up and smiled. "Your turn." But the smile didn't last long. High above, Skylor could see Dareth and Captain Soto making their third jump. They landed all wrong and Captain Soto went over the side, dangling from Dareth's outstretched arm.

"Let me go, lad, and save yourself!" cried the pirate.

"Don't be silly," said Dareth. "Just hang on and I'll pull you up."

"Good," said Soto. "Because I didn't really mean that!"

Above, Misako had found it surprising that she had made it a third of the way down to the ground without injury. Shaking off Echo Zane, she said, "I've got this," and jumped. But the rock was rising faster than she expected, and she missed it completely.

Plummeting toward the ground, Misako bounced off one rock, then another, but it didn't slow her down much. She closed her eyes and prepared herself for impact. She was halfway through the list of all the things she still wanted to do with her life when she felt a hand close around her wrist.

Misako opened her eyes to see Master Wu smiling down at her. "Spinjitzu," said Wu. "A most useful skill to learn."

Wu and Misako landed beside the others. All around them were huge craters, which were all that remained after Nadakhan had torn the land free from the planet's surface. They had survived, but they had not stopped the evil djinn.

"You have done well," Master Wu said to the team. "You have helped the people of the city, and you have lived to fight another day."

Ronin looked up at the sea of rock floating to the sky. "So what do we do if the ninja beat Nadakhan and it suddenly starts raining rocks?"

Master Wu followed his gaze. "We honor the courage of my ninja by matching it with our own. In life, Ronin, whatever goes up, must come down . . . and the job of a hero is to catch it when it falls."

THE LAST WISH

By Greg Farshtey

Master Wu and a ragtag group of warriors have saved the city, but in the sky above, Nya is now wedded to the terrible djinn Nadakhan, whose magic powers make him unstoppable. How can you stop the unstoppable? Impossible, right? Only the ninja Jay is left to tell the tale. Literally, he is going to tell the tale. Right now. In his own words . . .

"If wishes were lizards, we'd all be riding on dragons," my mom used to say.

Everyone has a wish they would love to come true. But when you run into someone like Nadakhan, who grants wishes and turns them against you, you're better off keeping your dreams to yourself. My name's Jay, and I'm the Lightning Ninja. No one will probably ever get to read this story, except maybe Nya.

What happened in the end is a big secret, but I'm starting this from the point when everything was going Nadakhan's way. He was ripping up chunks of Ninjago's land and levitating them to build a new world in the sky to rule from. He had captured Nya and was planning to marry her, and that made me angrier than I had ever been before.

I managed to crash the wedding at the djinn's temple with the rest of the ninja team, but we were too late—the ceremony was over. Nya and Nadakhan were married. (I think someone already said this, but: Yuck!)

We wound up fighting a bunch of magical duplicates of Nadakhan, but not the big bad guy himself. I was taking what I thought might be my last look at Nya when one of the pirates named Clancee told me about Tiger Widow venom, which might stop Nadakhan. And better yet, there was some hidden on their flying ship, *Misfortune's Keep*.

You see, Clancee and a few of the other pirates realized that Nadakhan was more than bad news. If he became ruler of the world, their pirating days would be over at best.

"And we did not want to think about what 'at worst' would mean for us!" Clancee said.

With the help of Flintlocke and Dogshank, two of the pirates who had turned against Nadakhan, the ninjas and I fought our way onto the flying ship. I found the Tiger Widow poison. Flintlocke volunteered to take a shot at Nadakhan with a venom-tipped dart when the time came.

Then all we had to do was get back to the djinn's temple. I had an idea for how to do that. . . .

"Come about, mateys!" I yelled in my best pirate-speak. "And dive! Straight at the temple!"

I was standing on the bow, the wind rushing past me, as *Misfortune's Keep* plummeted toward the temple. I liked to think that Nadakhan saw us coming, and knew all his plans were about to be smashed to smithereens. Probably not, but one thing I knew for sure: after what he had put my friends through, the djinn was mine. I was going to make sure he had granted his last evil wish.

Down below, pirate cannons were hurling cannonballs up at us. Sometimes it seemed the sky was just a bunch of solid black balls heading in our direction. It looked like a bowling alley had exploded. Misfortune's Keep took some bad hits, but they really knew how to build ships in the old days—it just kept flying.

At the last possible second, I yelled, "Hold on!"

The ninjas and the rest of the crew did the same. In the next instant, the ship smashed into the roof of the temple with a roar that drowned out everything else. The impact rattled our spines and threatened to shake our livers and other important organs loose.

Have you ever crashed a giant ship into a stone building? I wouldn't recommend it.

At first, all I could see were clouds of smoke. The dust was so thick, I could hardly breathe. But I got to my feet and saw that my friends were OK. And when I saw Nadakhan standing beside Nya, I was ready to fight.

"Looks like we crashed your party," Kai said to the djinn.

"And to think we forgot to bring a wedding gift," said Cole.

"I brought a little something," I added, drawing my sword. To Nya, I said, **"Step away from him. This guy's about to become French toast."**

Even as I said it, I knew something was wrong. It was her eyes. They weren't the eyes of the Nya I knew. They were hard and cold, like ice floating in a half-frozen sea . . . or like the expression in Master Wu's eyes when I used his teapot in my science experiments.

"My name is not Nya," she hissed. "It's Delara. And you'll pay for this."

"He has cast a spell on her," said Zane. "We must defeat him to save Nya."

Nadakhan looked me over like I was a little fish he was ready to throw back into the sea.

"You think you can cast me away with my own sword?" he said. "I wish you gone!"

I dived to the ground and the djinn bolt of magical energy passed over me. The other ninja started circling Nadakhan. The plan was simple: keep the djinn occupied and give Flintlocke time to take his shot.

Nadakhan had beaten us all individually, but we hoped for a better result as a group. It didn't look like it was going to make much difference, though.

"Ha-ha-ha-ha!" the cruel djinn laughed.

The djinn suddenly used his power to turn Zane to stone. Then he did the same thing to Cole and Kai. Lloyd lasted a few minutes more, but he was the next to go.

All of a sudden, I was the last ninja still made of flesh and bone. One of Nadakhan's blasts had separated me from my sword. Delara was laughing. Nadakhan seemed to be mere moments from victory. I was trying to think of something, anything, I could do . . . but the only thought in my head was that I had failed Nya.

"I wish—" Nadakhan began, with an evil gloating smile on his face.

That was when everything changed. Flintlocke took his shot—the dart struck Nadakhan, and the Tiger Widow venom splattered all over him. In the same moment, Nya returned to herself, and my friends changed from stone back into their normal selves. The djinn's power was fizzling out!

"The poison . . . it's working!" said Kai.

"Now, Jay!" yelled Cole. "Now!"

I knew what I was supposed to do. One wish, and Nadakhan would no longer be a threat to anyone. But as he stumbled and fell to his knees, I saw Nya behind him. The poison had splattered on her as well. I ran to her, and she collapsed into my arms.

"The poison hurts a djinn, but it will be fatal to her," said Zane.

Nadakhan looked up at me with a sneer. "You could save her with a wish, Jay. What a dilemma. Waste your wish fighting me, and she dies. Wish her well again, and there will be no stopping me."

I met Nya's eyes. She said, "You're the only one who can stop him."

"I can't let you go," I said softly.

"I never wanted to be part of your silly boys' club anyway," she replied with a weak chuckle. "I guess it's true that the greatest love stories always end in tragedy. . . ."

Her eyes slowly closed. I didn't notice Nadakhan getting to his feet behind me, raising his sword, ready to strike. It wouldn't have mattered if I had.

A thousand thoughts ran through my head in an instant, but my mind quickly settled on one of them—the teapot that had imprisoned Nadakhan for hundreds of years. I knew what I had to do.

"I wish . . . no one had ever found your teapot in the first place and that it stays lost forever and ever."

Nadakhan's smile of triumph faded. He looked at me, baffled. "Your wish . . . ? No . . . NO . . . N—"

I wasn't sure what would happen next. I guess the simple way to say it is that the world unraveled. Time turned back on itself, undoing all the events that had happened since Nadakhan was released from his teapot prison. No one would remember the levitating land masses, the sky pirate raids. None of it.

Well, almost no one . . .

Somehow, for reasons I'm not sure of, Nya and I remembered everything. Nadakhan was gone and everyone was safe, but the only thing that mattered to me was that my friend was alive . . . and that she didn't have to spend the rest of her life married to an evil djinn.

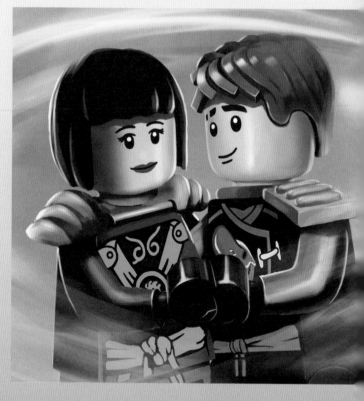

We decided not to tell the others what had happened. Everything had worked out, and it was a happy ending. Who could wish for anything more?

FRENEMIES

By Marta Leśniak

On a new mission, the ninja find themselves in trouble once again. Nya and Kai have fled from a dragon called Grief-Bringer, but they will soon face another problem. It will require the powers of the mind, body, and spirit to overcome. A spoon may also come in handy. Here's what happened. . . .

Kai, Nya, and the Geckle and Munce tribes were hiding in the Geckle Strong Cave.

"The dragon is blocking the way out," groaned Kai, whom the Geckles had chosen for their leader. "Plus we're stuck here with two battling tribes. And worse—no one delivers noodles here!"

"No noodles is definitely the worst part," Nya sighed, but

she knew there were more important things to worry about right now.

Nya, who had just been crowned the new Munce Queen, went to comfort her brother. A loud scream stopped her.

"This is my stone!" shouted a Munce. "It's mine now replied a Geckle, who had just carved a mark on the stone.

The Geckles and Munces continued to fuss and fight.

"I miss our dojo," Kai said, looking at the quarreling tribesmen. "I really want to go home."

"I know," Nya replied. "But we have to wait here until Grief-Bringer leaves."

"We'll go nuts because of their constant quarrelling," said Kai.

"No. We will get the tribes to call a truce once and for all," Nya answered. "I know it sounds impossible, but . . ."

". . . let's see if we can teach these two tribes how to get along," Kai said, finishing the thought. "Let's try it!"

The ninja decided that maybe the tribes would learn to cooperate if it they made it fun. They decided to teach them some of the games they had played as kids.

"Everybody!" Nya yelled. "Come over and sit down in a circle, a Geckle next to a Munce."

"We don't want the Geckles next to us," grumbled a Munce.

"The Munce smells odd," a Geckle complained.

"Quit whining and GET IN THE CIRCLE," snapped Kai, and the members of the two tribes quickly took a seat. "We'll play a game. I'll whisper a word to a person next to me, who will whisper it to his neighbor. You'll keep passing the word to the next person, until the Queen hears it and says it out loud."

The members of the tribes continued
to grumble, but eventually everyone got
comfortable. Kai leaned over to the nearest
Geckle and whispered, "Spinjitzu."

The game began, and the reluctant players passed the word to each other. Then it was Nya's turn. She tried, "MINJITZU?"

"Right!" the Munce shouted happily.

"Wrong!" protested the Geckle. "It should be GINJITZU!"

Kai laughed, but then another brawl broke out between the tribes. "I forgot," Kai groaned. "They love to twist words!"

"Don't worry—I've got another idea!" said Nya. "We'll
make pairs so that a Geckle and a Munce dance together.
We need music, so you'll sing. I will decide which pair wins."

"Time for everyone to show off their dance moves!" Kai
told the tribes, who were giving each other dirty looks.

Matching the Geckles and the Munce into pairs for dancing was not easy. But an hour later, the mixed partners were finally ready. Kai started to sing as the competition began.

Suddenly, a scream of pain echoed throughout the cave.

"OUUUCH! You clumsy ox!" shouted a Geckle, landing hard on the ground after he'd been thrown into the air by his Munce dance partner. His partner had forgotten to catch him.

"You're the clumsy ox!" the Munce snarled.

Meanwhile, another pair trampled each other's feet, one Geckle was dizzy from too many spins, and a Munce covered his ears when he heard Kai's singing.

It took only a moment for the two tribes to start yet another brawl.

"I'll go nuts if this keeps up," said Nya, sighing. It seemed there was nothing they could do to get them to put aside their differences.

"Can we have a lunch break?" Nya asked.

Too keep the tribes from fighting again,
Nya chose one Geckle and one Munce to
prepare the meal.

Soon loud noises could be heard from the kitchen. BANG! CRASH! TWANG! But it eventually went quiet, and a strange—and delightful, if you were a Munce or a Geckle—smell filled the cave. Finally, the proud cooks emerged, carrying cauldrons full of greenish mash.

"Best dish in the world!" cried the Geckles, smacking their lips.

"Oh, it's our favorite, too!" shouted the Munce.

"We didn't know we have the same taste in food!" one of them said as she placed a large portion of the mash before the ninja. "You'll love it, too."

The ninjas weren't so sure.

"Ugh! It smells like rotten cheese wrapped in dirty socks!" Kai whispered to Nya.

Both tribes started to feast on the smelly mash, wishing each other "Bon appétit."

"You eat it." Kai slid his bowl to Nya. "You were hungry."

"Not anymore!" Nya said in disgust, sliding the bowl back to her brother. "I'll wait for some noodles . . . no matter how long it takes."

"And they say we're the ones who keep quarrelling," said a Geckle, looking at the ninja fussing over the bowl while everyone else in the cave was enjoying their meal. Some were even going for second helpings.

"After lunch, we'll try to help them out," replied a Munce, sitting beside him. "Now let's enjoy the meal!"

THE LEGEND OF JAY

By Stacia Deutsch

The ninja enter a digital world like a video game, where they will have to win challenges and earn credits to prove their skills. It sounds easy, but if they lose the games, then . . . well, best not think about that! They're ninja. It will probably be okay. Probably. Ninja Jay goes first and find that the stakes are very real and the chance to play guitar like a rock star only requires evading capture and leading a successful rebellion. What? It could happen. You'll see. . . .

"**W**ould you like to enter the game Prime Empire?" the screen asked.

Jay, the Lightning Ninja, had quickly moved to Level 13 of the video game. Standing in an abandoned arcade while his friends explored the building, Jay eagerly pressed a button.

"Heck, yes!"

Suddenly, the game cabinet opened like a portal. Stepping inside, Jay found himself in a bustling city. Ultra-modern skyscrapers, brightly colored neon signs, cluttered shops packed with anything and everything a citizen of the video game city could want, crowds of oddly dressed people—everything was overwhelming.

"Welcome to Prime Empire," said a man who watched Jay from a shop nearby.

"Prime Empire?" Jay couldn't believe he was in the game! It was real!

The man beckoned Jay into his shop. "Whoa!" Jay looked in awe at the skateboards, comic books, and gaming gadgets on the shelves. "This shop is so cool! I want everything! And I want that, too!" He pointed at an electric guitar hanging on a wall. The glowing strings crackled with energy.

"That's expensive. You might want to check your credits," said the shopkeeper, showing him how.

Jay opened a hologram with his stats. "Zero?"

"Come back when you get credits," the man replied.

"How do I get—" Jay began. Just then, loud sirens blared and images of his face appeared on video screens, declaring him to be wanted by the video game authorities. Instantly, an army of security robots swarmed the streets.

"Uh-oh! Red Visors! Looks like you're in trouble, stranger," warned the shopkeeper.

"Huh? What did I do?" Jay cried as he hurried outside. People ducked and hid as the Red Visors marched toward Jay. Red Visors were simple robots—enforcers in the digital world. Unlike the other players, the robot didn't have to follow the rules. They made the game more fun, and more dangerous, too.

Jay quickly realized there was no way he could fight the robots all by himself. He had to run and hide! Jay saw a parked race car and snuck into the trunk. Through a crack he watched a man battle some Red Visors before jumping into the driver's seat and taking off.

But two vehicles driven by Red Visors appeared out of nowhere. The man made a few tricky maneuvers that took their robots' vehicles out of the game. It seemed that the pursuit was over, but a third vehicle suddenly crashed right into the race car, sending Jay sprawling onto the street.

The driver was stunned to see who his stowaway was. He made sure Jay was OK, then helped him get up. "My name's Scott. I've been waiting for you a long time."

"Do I know you?" Jay was confused.

"No time to explain. We gotta get out of here!" Scott glanced at his wrecked car and added, "Come on!"

Scott led Jay to an empty car parked a few streets away. Once they got into it, Scott pressed a button and a building appeared. "I've got a Level 999 Stealth Barrier on my garage,"  he bragged. "No one can see us here, not even—"

He stopped when they heard several small explosions outside.

"The rebels are fighting the Red Visors," he explained. "Prime Empire's freedom is at stake."

"We can help them!" Jay exclaimed. "Like you helped me."

"Too risky for me." Scott revealed his stats. "I've only got one life left."

Jay considered what his ninja friends would do in his place. Without hesitation, Jay left the safety of Scott's hideout and ran to join the rebels battling the Red Visors.

"Look! It's Jay!" a voice shouted. "We've been waiting for you," one of the rebels declared with a wide smile. Jay thought that was weird. Scott had said the same thing.

"Jay, look out!" a rebel shouted. A Red Visor was coming fast, about to attack.

Jay took a defensive stance. "Time for you to taste some Spinjitzu! Nin-jaaa-go!" he yelled. But instead of creating a mighty spin, his leg kicked clumsily and faltered.

"You have no powers here," called another rebel as he fought off a Red Visor.

"Disappointing!" Jay groaned. "Now what?"

"We're outnumbered. We have to retreat. Follow me." Another rebel showed Jay how to jump once, then again. He landed on a high rooftop.

"Double jump? Classic game move!" Jay popped onto the same roof.

Many roofs later, Jay and the rebels were safe—and away from the Red Visors.

"Whoa, jumping is exhausting!" Jay was fighting for breath.

"Low stamina," one of the rebels explained. "We'll show you ways to earn stamina."

"I need to earn credits, too," Jay said. "There's an awesome guitar I want. . . ."

The rebels took Jay on many skill-shaping missions. Jay rescued a cat by quadruple-jumping up a tree.

"Good deeds get credits!" he declared.

He crushed boulders with his bare fists. "Stamina gained with hard work."

He and the rebels defeated some train robbers by flipping, kicking, and punching. "Bonus skills earned by saving the day!" Jay cheered as he checked his status.

Jay and the gang were on their way back to the hideout when they passed the shop. Jay stopped there, dreamily looking at the guitar. He sighed. "Soon you'll be mine!"

But there was something even more important on Jay's mind. "You taught me how to survive in Prime Empire," he said to the rebels. "How can I repay you?"

"We need a leader," a rebel replied. "We'd be honored if it was you."

"I gotta get back to my friends," Jay replied, looking sad. "Ninjago world needs me."

The rebels were heartbroken. "Farewell, then, Hero Jay," they said. And one by one, they slid down a manhole into their hideout.

Jay didn't realize a Red Visor was watching them the whole time.

"I've located the rebel lair! Send troops!" the robot called.

As the Red Visors flooded the street, Jay realized he'd accidentally shown them the rebel hideout! Even with his improved stats, there were still too many robots to fight alone. Jay was helpless. He ran to Scott's garage as fast as he could.

"Red Visors stormed the hideout and took the rebels somewhere!" he cried.

"The Red Visors probably took the rebels to prison," Scott said. "If you want to help them, we need to go . . . shopping."

To Jay's surprise, Scott took him to the store he already knew very well.

"This console produces any weapon you'll need. In a ninja's hand, it'll be devastating," the shopkeeper assured Jay.

"Devastating is my middle name! I'll take it. And that cool outfit, too." The ninja pointed at some blue armor. The items cost Jay almost all his credits. He put the armor on and looked at the guitar for the last time. "So long forever, my darling."

The grim prison building was just a few streets away, and Jay quickly made his way there.

Jay laid out the plan to Scott. "I take the guards down, then we get in and set the rebels free. Easy! Stay behind me, and I'll protect your one life."

"Thanks." Scott smiled. "Let's go before I change my mind."

Jay pressed a button, and when his new console produced mighty energy nunchucks, he charged the robots. The vicious Red Visors swarmed Jay, but the ninja wasn't afraid as he whirled the nunchucks. Red Visor after Red Visor fell, never seeing what hit them.

Jay and Scott opened the prison cells and the rebels ran free.

"We knew you wouldn't leave us!" the rebels cheered.

"We've won!" Jay declared. The rebels cheered again.

Scott offered the rebels a new lair attached by a tunnel to his garage. "I'll install the Level 999 Stealth Barrier. If there are anymore Red Visors roaming around, they won't be able to find us. Tonight we celebrate!"

Later, in the new rebel lair, there was an epic party.

"We have a present for you," one of the rebels said. The lights flashed, and suddenly everyone was dressed like Jay. "We are the League of Jay!"

"Wow! This is . . . w-weird," Jay stuttered. "But I like it!"

Then a rebel Jay handed the real Jay the guitar he wanted.

"Oh! Can this get any better?" Jay was deeply moved. He wished his ninja team could see him now. He began to play, and as an awesome riff hit the air, he changed into a cool rock star.

"You're Superstar Rockin' Jay now!" the League of Jay cheered. "Jay-jaaaa-GO!"

Before leaving the game, Jay partied with all his new friends!

LOOK BEFORE YOU LEAP!

By Steve Behling

While Jay rocked into the night with his new friends, the other ninja face other challenges in the video game world. The digital city is fast-paced and dangerous. Kai and Cole are going to have to move just as quickly if they want to survive!

"Is this even a game?" Kai said. "It looks like rush hour in Ninjago City!"

Kai, the Fire Ninja, and Cole, the Earth Ninja, had entered a portal and appeared inside a new game. They stood on the sidewalk in front of a busy street. Cars, trucks, and buses zoomed by. Beyond the street, Kai saw another sidewalk. And beyond that was

another street with even more speeding vehicles. Before Cole could reply, another player appeared next to him. He was wearing knights' armor and carried a sword.

"Hey! I see you're playing Super Cross the Road and Don't Get Squashed, too!" the player said.

"Wait, the game is called what, now?" Kai said.

The new player jumped into the street, dashed between a sports car and a motorcycle, then leapt onto the sidewalk on the other side.

"It's easy!" he shouted. "See? Just jump between the vehicles without getting squashed."

"I can't play this game, Cole," Kai protested. "I only have one life left!"

"We don't have a choice," Cole said. "We'll never get out of this digital world if we don't play! Besides, the game doesn't look that hard. Look at the new guy!"

The new player smiled at Kai and Cole. A fire truck whizzed by as he stepped into the street. But before he could jump onto the next sidewalk, he was run over by a giant toy duck!

"So it's a little more complicated than it looks," Cole said as the knight reappeared next to them.

"It's, uh, tricky," the knight said as he jumped into traffic again—and was promptly flattened by a donut-shaped car. This time he didn't reappear.

"He ran out of lives," Kai said. "That could be me!"

"If we don't play, we can forget the race," Cole insisted. "You can do this, Kai."

Kai shook his head, then looked up at Cole.

"I know," he said. "We have to be careful. Stick together. No showing off. Get the points and get out. Agreed?"

"Agreed," Cole said. To Kai's horror, he jumped right into the street.

"That was being careful?" Kai said, following
Cole into the digital traffic, where they narrowly
escaped getting clipped by a runaway hot-dog
cart before making it to the opposite sidewalk.

"Sorry," Cole said. "I know we need to be careful,
but with our skills . . . I think we got this!"

"I hope you're right," Kai replied. "Otherwise, it's
bye-bye, credits."

Cole stared ahead at the traffic. A double-decker bus drove by, followed by a steamroller, then a clown riding a unicycle. As soon as they had passed, another double-decker bus, another steamroller, and another clown riding a unicycle went by.

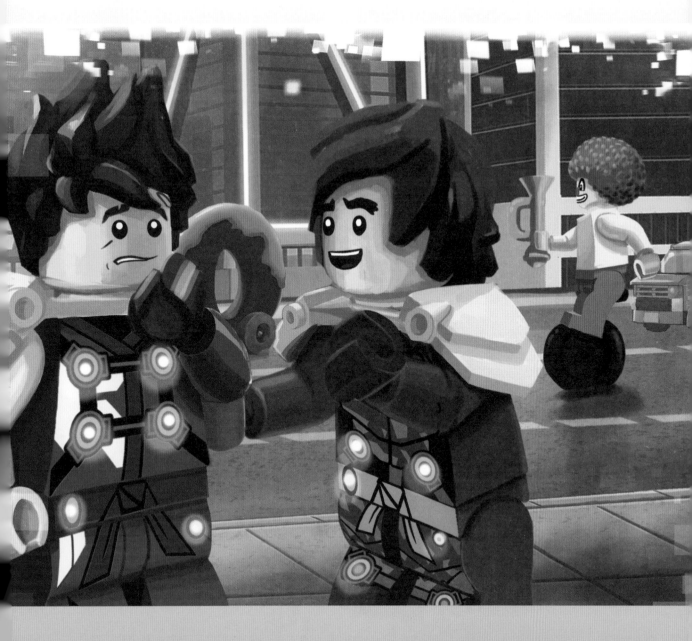

"There's a pattern," Cole said. "Let the clown pass. Then we can jump into the street and over to the next sidewalk."

"Are you sure?" Kai asked. "It didn't work out so well for that other player."

"He didn't know the pattern," Cole said. "We do."

"All right," Kai said. "But we do it together this time, okay? On your mark. One. Two—"

"Three!" Cole shouted, and the two ninja leapt into the busy street. The clown on the unicycle passed, honking his horn. There was just enough time for them to jump onto the next sidewalk before the double-decker bus came barreling down the road.

"We made it!" Kai said. "Now what?"

Both ninja stared at a wide, flowing river ahead. Logs floated by—some drifted left to right, while others moved from right to left. Past the logs was a row of sleeping bears.

"We have to jump across," Kai said.

"And find the pattern," said Cole. He watched intently, trying to judge the perfect moment for them to jump onto the logs.

"You know what's weird?" Cole asked.

"What?" Kai replied. "Other than every single thing we've encountered?"

"There's no time limit on this game," Cole said. "Like, shouldn't there be a clock or something?"

"There is no clock because you're already out of time," came a voice from above.

"Who said that?" Cole demanded.

All at once, a squadron of Red Visors—mindless robots that enforced the video game world's rules—appeared behind them. They aimed their blasters at Kai and Cole!

There was no time to figure out the pattern. Cole dodged the Red Visors' blasts, landing on a floating log. A Red Visor joined him and the log began to spin. Cole kept his balance, but the Red Visor wasn't so lucky. The robot fell into the water, disappearing in a shower of sparks!

"Mental note!" Kai called out. "Do not hit the river!"

Kai followed Cole and jumped atop a log with another Red Visor. "I don't like being chased," Kai said, flinging the robot into the water.

"What about the bears?" Kai shouted. The bears were no longer floating on their backs. They were now awake, their claws bared. They swiped at Kai and Cole.

"I have an idea," Kai said.

Cole wasn't sure what his friend had in mind. He knew Kai tended to act before thinking, and that could spell trouble. But he also trusted Kai.

"I'm with you," Cole said. Before he knew it, Kai had grabbed him by the arms and was twirling him around. He threw Cole right over the angry bears! Then Kai leapt into the air. Somersaulting, he bounced off a bear's head!

The Red Visors tried to follow, but they were batted away by the snarling bears.

"So far, so good!" Cole said.

The ninja were nearly at the other side of the river when suddenly, an enormous shark popped out of the water.

"You call this good?" Kai shouted.

"Could be worse," Cole said as they landed on the shark's back. The shark shook the ninja, throwing them high into the air. Then it opened its mouth, ready to catch them in its gaping maw.

"It's worse," Kai said.

"Maybe not," Cole said as they continued to fall. "Grab my hands!"

Kai looked at his friend and smiled. He could always count on Cole—this ninja would never let anyone down. He took Cole's hands.

"We'll take him out together . . . from inside!" Cole ordered. "Watch out for the teeth, though!"

For a split second, Kai thought Cole was out of his mind! But then he reminded himself that his friend had trusted him before. Could Kai do any less for him now?

So the two ninja, holding hands, dived right into the shark's mouth. A moment later, the shark's eyes went wide. BURRRP! The creature let out a belch.

Then it exploded!

Both Cole and Kai were sent flying. They landed on the other side of the river with the only part of the shark that was left—its fin.

"We did it!" Kai cheered.

"Of course we did, but don't you ever tell anyone how we did it," Cole said. "Now let's collect those credits and get out of here!"

A FRIEND IN NEED

By Steve Behling

While Kai and Cole successfully completed their game challenge, Lloyd faced his video game alone. Well, except for the fact that he runs into an old friend—and some old enemies So his game is really dangerous, but at least he is not really alone. . . .

"OK, this is weird!" Lloyd said as a digital alien blasted at him. "And dangerous!"

He had entered the game Triple Attack, hoping to win credits that would enable him to win the game. But at the moment, rows of alien invaders fired laser blasts from above. They descended faster and faster, getting closer and closer.

Dodging blasts, Lloyd ran beneath a large mushroom-shaped shelter.

"How am I gonna beat this game on my own?" Lloyd asked.

"You are not alone," came a familiar voice.

A surprised Lloyd turned to see the samurai Okino. Okino was a powerful warrior known for his bravery. The ninjas had met the samurai before, and they had been on other adventures together. Okino was a reliable comrade.

"Okino!" Lloyd exclaimed. "What are you doing here?"

"I am following my own path," Okino said. "And that path has brought me here. And now we fight. Together."

Okino reached into his tunic and handed something to Lloyd.

"A throwing star?" Lloyd said, looking at the object.

"Follow my lead." Okino was holding his own throwing star. "On the count of three. One. Two—"

"THREE!" Lloyd finished. They hurled the stars at the aliens. The creatures exploded into balls of blue light! Then the stars returned to Lloyd and Okino.

"Whoa! Boomerang stars!" Lloyd said. "We can't lose if we throw them fast enough!"

"Do not be overconfident," Okino said.

But Lloyd was already busy throwing his boomerang star at other aliens, eliminating one after another. Then a bigger and faster alien zoomed in. Lloyd threw his star at it. Instead of exploding, the alien absorbed the weapon with a loud gulp!

"Uh-oh," said Lloyd.

The aliens approached as Okino threw his own
star to Lloyd. The samurai plucked a mushroom
from the ground and hurled it at the alien that
had eaten Lloyd's star.

The alien disappeared!

"Why didn't you say something about the
mushrooms before?" Lloyd said, starting to throw
mushrooms, too.

"Because I only just discovered them!" Okino replied with a self-assured grin.

Using the mushrooms, the two warriors made quick work of the remaining aliens.

"Woo-hoo! We did it!" Lloyd said. "High five time, my friend! We won!"

"No," Okino said grimly. "This was only . . . the beginning!"

"How do you know?" Lloyd asked.

"The game is called Triple Attack," Okino said. "This was but the first. That means there are two more to come."

"Yoo-hoo! Ho!"

Lloyd looked up at a hovering platform that
appeared above them with a band of creatures on
it. He recognized the furry creatures in an instant.
It was the Brotherhood of Rats! But what were
they doing in the game?

"You!" Lloyd shouted, pointing at the dirty rats. "You dirty rats!"

"Yeah, yeah, it's us!" replied one of them. "And we're in control of this game!"

"Oooh-hooo!" another rat laughed. "Get ready to be destroyed by . . . BEACH BALLS!"

"Did you just say beach balls?" Lloyd asked, scratching his head. That didn't sound so bad.

"I did!" the rat replied. Suddenly, the sky shimmered, and row after row of bright red, yellow, and blue beach balls dropped to the ground! When they hit, they flattened whatever they touched. Mushrooms went SPLAT! The balls then bounced back into the sky.

"If we get hit, we'll end up like those mushrooms!" Lloyd said.

Okino nodded. "Only if we don't move," he said. "So move!"

A beach ball fell to the ground, and Lloyd and Okino barely had time to leap out of its way as they landed on top of their mushroom shelter.

"Give up now!" a rat snarled. "And maybe we'll only squash you a little!"

Okino glared at the rats. "Never!" he said. "Let's see how these beach balls fare against my steel!"

Unsheathing his samurai sword, Okino slashed at a beach ball. It hissed air and then disappeared!

"Use your blade!" Okino shouted.

"You don't have to tell me twice!" Lloyd said.

In the time it had taken Lloyd to draw his katana, Okino had sliced three more beach balls. Lloyd slashed at a beach ball, making it disappear, but it had taken some effort. Okino made it look so easy!

"We got this," Lloyd said.

"Yes," Okino said. "But as long as the Brotherhood of Rats controls the game, it will never end. We must stop them!"

The platform landed on the ground as the rats decided to change their strategy. One of them grinned cheekily and pressed a big red button. The ground began to rumble, and a giant snake appeared with enormous fangs in its mouth.

"What devilry is this?" Okino said.

"Are you blind or what? It's a snake!" the rat said. "A really big snake! And it's gonna eat you!"

"Not if I can do something about it!" replied Okino. He turned to Lloyd. "Remember, the snake is not our enemy. The rats control the game. The rats are our enemy! Distract the snake! Leave the rest to me."

Lloyd nodded and screamed at the snake, "Hey! Big and ugly! Over here!"

The snake slithered straight at Lloyd. Okino snuck in from the side and sliced the snake in two with one swift cut of his sword!

But the snake didn't disappear. Instead, the second piece grew another head. Now there were two slithering snakes!

"Hmm . . ." Okino said. "That was *not* my plan."

"All right, then: Plan B," Lloyd said. He took aim with his last boomerang star, and threw it at the first snake. The star split it in two. That part grew a head. Now there were three snakes!

"Ha!" a rat shouted. "That's the sound of me laughin'!"

"Perhaps the mushrooms . . . ?" Okino suggested. He reached down, plucked some mushrooms, and hurled them at the snakes. The creatures turned their heads, catching and eating the mushrooms.

The snakes grew larger!

"Plan C. Run!" Okino yelled as the three snakes headed for them. But before the snakes could strike, they managed to get out of the way—just as all three snakes collided in a huge explosion of smoke. When the smoke cleared, there was only one snake . . . except it was three times as big!

"Enough of it! We must stop playing the rats' game, and play our own," Okino said firmly. "Let's take this game to the rats!"

"I know what you're thinking," Lloyd said.

The ninja and the samurai smiled at each other and ran for the rats. The giant snake followed.

"Ha! Look at 'em run!" said one of the rats, laughing.

"Yeah! They're runnin' right at us! Oooo-hoo! Ha! Ha!" laughed another.

But the rats were too busy having fun to see what Lloyd and Okino were up to. At the last possible second, the warriors jumped out of the way and the snake crashed into the rats, destroying their platform! The snake disappeared instantly, and the game ended.

"You did it!" Lloyd said. "You beat the rats and won the credits!"

"No," Okino answered. "We did it. And those credits are yours."

"Thank you, my friend. But what about you?" Lloyd asked.

"As always, I must follow my own path, Lloyd. Just as you must follow yours. I hope our paths cross again someday, my friend."

The ninja and the samurai bowed to one another as Lloyd exited the game.

HOUSE OF HORRORS!

By Steve Behling

Now that the other ninjas have won their games, it is up to Jay and Nya to win the final—and most terrifying—game. Will their individual successes bring the ninja closer to their goal? Or will it be game over for the Elemental Masters?

"Hey, Nya," Jay said. "Remind me why you picked the Haunted House?"

"*We* picked the game, remember?" the Water Ninja answered.

The two ninja had entered the mini game and were standing in front of an old house with boarded-up windows. Dark clouds hung above, and bats circled the spikes of the pointed roof.

"Come on," Nya laughed. "We just have to walk through the house and out the back door. It's a piece of cake!"

Jay shook his head. "This is not a piece of cake," he said. "I like cake. Cake is delicious. This is not cake. This is . . . spooky."

On the word "spooky," lightning flashed overhead.

"See?" Jay said, pointing at the lightning.

The ninja walked up the old steps to the front door and pushed it open. The door let out a loud creak as Jay and Nya entered the house. Inside, they saw a grand entranceway with a large staircase in the center and burning candles on either side. Cobwebs covered the walls.

"Yikes," Jay said.

"Wait, is the Lightning Ninja afraid of a haunted house?" Nya said with a laugh. "C'mon, I'll go first, chicken."

"I'm not chicken," Jay said, following Nya. "I'm just cautious!"

"Let's just breeze through the bottom floor and get out," Nya said.

Suddenly, all the open doors in all the hallways closed shut with a loud simultaneous SLAM!

"I don't think they want us down here," Jay said. "Whoever 'they' are."

"Then I guess we take the stairs," Nya said. "Maybe there's a way out up there."

Nya started up the stairs as Jay followed. A moment later, he felt an icy hand grab his shoulder.

Jay turned around slowly to look at the pale hand resting on his shoulder. It belonged to an elegantly dressed man in a black suit and cape, with dark slicked-back hair, glowing red eyes, and creepy fangs.

"You're a vampire, right?" Jay gulped. "Indeed," the vampire said. "Welcome to my house. Be my guest . . . forever!"

The vampire lunged at Jay. He was going to bite the ninja! Jay ducked. He kicked out a leg, swiping at the vampire and knocking him down the stairs.

"Nya, run!" Jay yelled as the vampire quickly got to his feet, shaking cobwebs from his cape.

The ninja ran down the hall, leaping over gaps in the rotting floorboards until they came to a door at the end.

"You cannot escape!" the vampire snarled at the ninja.

"Open it!" Jay said. "The vampire's almost here!"

"What do you think I'm doing?" Nya shot back as she opened the door. The ninja pushed into the room, slamming the door closed.

Jay whirled around and was stunned at the sight of a real desert and a life-sized pyramid! But more troubling was the army of mummies lumbering toward them. There must have been a hundred! Wrapped in bandages, the monsters shuffled closer. Savage-looking scorpions emerged from the sand and followed, claws snapping.

"There's got to be a way out of here," Nya said, swiping away scorpions.

"Yeah, the door," Jay replied. "And there's a vampire behind it, remember?"

WHOOSH! A mummy threw a punch at Jay. But the ninja ducked, grabbing some loose wrappings that dangled from the creature. With a YANK, Jay pulled, spinning the mummy around. The wrappings unraveled—leaving nothing but dust and sand.

"Not so scary now, are you?" Jay said.

"Keep fighting!" Nya shouted.

The ninja kicked mummies, pulled on wrappings, and dodged scorpion stings.

"Nya, look!" Jay hollered. A door had opened in the pyramid.

"Go for it!" Nya exclaimed.

The ninja sprinted for the door as the
mummies and scorpions followed. Leaping inside,
they were surprised to find themselves back in
the hallway. Slowly, the hallway began to rotate,
and Jay and Nya fell onto a wall that had
become the floor.

"You should never have come here!" a haunting voice shrieked loudly. "You will be trapped here forever. . . . "

The hallway started to rotate again, and now the ninja were sitting on the ceiling.

"With me!" the voice finished with a terrible laugh.

"He must be controlling this house!" Jay said. "Well, you're doing a terrible job, because we're gonna win this game!"

"Are you?" the voice said. "Let's see how you fare against *these* horrors!"

Suddenly, the doors on either side of the upside-down hallway opened, releasing a horde of ghoulish monsters! **There were zombies and swamp creatures, a Frankenstein's monster and ghosts, and werewolves and witches.** Then the hallway began to rotate once more. But this time it didn't stop. It was constantly turning! The ninja ran headlong into the charging monsters. They jumped from the ceiling to the wall to the floor, trying to avoid tricky cracks and holes while also dodging a Frankenstein's monster's grasp, a swamp creature's claws, and a werewolf's fangs.

The big green fist of a Frankenstein's monster almost hit Jay, but he slid right under the punch. One by one, the monsters fell, until the ninja had reached a door at the end of the hallway. They opened it and stepped back in horror.

"Hello again," the vampire sneered. "Did you miss me? It was rather rude of you to slam the door on me before. Now prepare to meet your doom!"

The vampire swiped a claw at Jay—but Nya swatted the monster's hand away.

"Argh!" the vampire snarled. "I'll get you yet!"

There was another POOF of gray mist, and the vampire disappeared. But in his place was a large, sinister bat!

"I know what to do with this guy," Jay said, grabbing the bat. He hurled the creature into one of the holes in the floor, then grabbed Nya's hand and they both rushed to the door. Before the bat could fly out of the hole, the ninja escaped through the door and quickly slammed it without looking back.

Jay and Nya fell against some tall weeds and raggedy bushes outside the old house. They watched in surprise as the house shuddered for a moment, then began to collapse into itself. The ground rumbled, and soo there was nothing left of the haunted house.

"Phew! It's over, right?" Jay sighed. "I think I've had enough games for a while."

"No time to rest yet," said Nya. "Let's get our credits and get out of here. We may have survived our game, but we have to make sure the others are all right!"

"Of course they're all right," Jay said with a smile. "We're ninjas. We're masters of the Elemental Powers, and we always come out on top!"